D1146098

THE FOLLOWERS

The Followers

A Story by Dylan Thomas
with illustrations by Meg Stevens

J. M. Dent   London

Previously published in the volume
A Prospect of the Sea and Other Stories and Prose Writing, 1955
First published in this edition 1976
Reprinted 1994

Printed in Italy

It was six o'clock on a winter's evening.
Thin, dingy rain spat and drizzled past the
lighted street lamps. The pavements shone long
and yellow. In squeaking goloshes, with
mackintosh collars up and bowlers and
trilbies weeping, youngish men from the offices
bundled home against the thistly wind—

'Night, Mr Macey.'

'Going my way, Charlie?'

'Ooh, there's a pig of a night!'

'Good night, Mr Swan.'—
and older men, clinging on to the big, black circular birds
of their umbrellas, were wafted back, up the gaslit hills,
to safe, hot, slippered, weatherproof hearths, and wives called
Mother, and old, fond, fleabag dogs, and the wireless
babbling.

Young women from the offices, who smelt of scent and
powder and wet pixie hoods and hair, scuttled, giggling,
arm-in-arm, after the hissing trams, and screeched as they
splashed their stockings in the puddles rainbowed with oil
between the slippery lines.

In a shop window, two girls
undressed the dummies:

'Where you going to-night?'

'Depends on Arthur. Up she
comes.'

'Mind her cami-knicks,
Edna . . .'

The blinds came down over
another window.

A newsboy stood in a doorway,
calling the news to nobody,
very softly:

'Earthquake. Earthquake in
Japan.'

Water from a chute dripped on to his sacking. He waited in his own pool of rain.

A flat, long girl drifted, snivelling into her hanky, out of a jeweller's shop, and slowly pulled the steel shutters down with a hooked pole. She looked, in the grey rain, as though she were crying from top to toe.

A silent man and woman, dressed in black, carried the wreaths away from the front of their flower shop into the scented deadly darkness behind the window lights. Then the lights went out.

A man with a balloon tied to his cap pushed a shrouded barrow up a dead end.

A baby with an ancient face sat in its pram outside the wine vaults, quiet, very wet, peering cautiously all round it.

It was the saddest evening I had ever known.

A young man, with his arm round his girl, passed by me, laughing; and she laughed back, right into his handsome, nasty face. That made the evening sadder still.

I met Leslie at the corner of Crimea Street. We were both about the same age: too young and too old. Leslie carried a rolled umbrella, which he never used, though sometimes he pressed doorbells with it. He was trying to grow a moustache. I wore a check, ratting cap at a Saturday angle.

We greeted each other formally:

'Good evening, old man.'

'Evening, Leslie.'

'Right on the dot, boy.'

'That's right,' I said. 'Right on the dot.'

A plump, blonde girl, smelling of wet rabbits, selfconscious even in that dirty night, minced past on high-heeled shoes. The heels clicked, the soles squelched.

Leslie whistled after her, low and admiring.

'Business first,' I said.

'Oh, boy!' Leslie said.

'And she's too fat as well.'

'I like them corpulent,' Leslie said. 'Remember Penelope Bogan? a Mrs too.'

'Oh, come *on*. That old bird or Paradise Alley! How's the exchequer, Les?'

'One and a penny. How you fixed?'

'Tanner.'

'What'll it be, then? The Compasses?'

'Free cheese at the Marlborough.'

We walked towards the Marlborough, dodging umbrella spokes, smacked by our windy macs, stained by steaming lamplight, seeing the sodden, blown scourings and street⁄wash of the town, papers, rags, dregs, rinds, fag⁄ends, balls of fur, flap, float, and cringe along the gutters, hearing the sneeze and rattle of the bony trams and a ship hoot like a fog⁄ditched owl in the bay, and Leslie said:

'What'll we do after?'

'We'll follow someone,' I said.

'Remember following that old girl up Kitchener Street? The one who dropped her handbag?'

'You should have given it back.'

'There wasn't anything in it, only a piece of bread⁄and⁄jam.'

'Here we are,' I said.

The Marlborough saloon was cold and empty. There were notices on the damp walls: No Singing. No Dancing. No Gambling. No Peddlers.

'You sing,' I said to Leslie, 'and I'll dance, then we'll have a game of nap and I'll peddle my braces.'

The barmaid, with gold hair and two gold teeth in front, like a well-off rabbit's, was blowing on her nails and polishing them on her black marocain. She looked up as we came in, then blew on her nails again and polished them without hope.

'You can tell it isn't Saturday night,' I said. 'Evening, Miss. Two pints.'

'And a pound from the till,' Leslie said.

'Give us your one-and-a-penny, Les,' I whispered and then said aloud: 'Anybody can tell it isn't Saturday night. Nobody sick.'

'Nobody here to *be* sick,' Leslie said.

The peeling, liver-coloured room might never have been drunk in at all. Here, commercials told jokes and had Scotches and sodas with happy, dyed, port-and-lemon women; dejected regulars grew grand and muzzy in the corners, inventing their pasts, being rich, important and

loved; reprobate grannies in dustbin black cackled and
nipped; influential nobodies revised the earth; a party, with
earrings, called 'Frilly Willy' played the crippled piano,
which sounded like a hurdy-gurdy playing under water, until
the publican's nosy wife said, 'No.' Strangers came and went,
but mostly went. Men from the valleys dropped in for nine or
ten; sometimes there were fights; and always there was something doing, some argie-bargie, giggle and bluster, horror or
folly, affection, explosion, nonsense, peace, some wild goose
flying in the boozy air of that comfortless, humdrum nowhere
in the dizzy, ditchwater town at the end of the railway lines.
But that evening it was the saddest room I had ever known.

Leslie said, in a low voice: 'Think she'll let us have one on
tick?'

'Wait a bit, boy,' I murmured. 'Wait for her to thaw.'

But the barmaid heard me, and looked up. She looked clean through me, back through my small history to the bed I was born in, then shook her gold head.

'I don't know what it is,' said Leslie as we walked up Crimea Street in the rain, 'but I feel kind of depressed to-night.'

'It's the saddest night in the world,' I said.

We stopped, soaked and alone, to look at the stills outside the cinema we called the Itch-pit. Week after week, for years and years, we had sat on the edges of the springless seats there, in the dank but snug, flickering dark, first with toffees and monkey-nuts that crackled for the dumb guns, and then with cigarettes: a cheap special kind that would make a fire-swallower cough up the cinders of his heart. 'Let's go in and see Lon Chaney,' I said, 'and Richard Talmadge and Milton Sills and . . . and Noah Beery,' I said, 'and Richard Dix . . . and Slim Summerville and Hoot Gibson.'

We both sighed.

'Oh, for our vanished youth,'
I said.

We walked on heavily,
with wilful feet, splashing the
passers-by.

'Why don't you open your
brolly?' I said.

'It won't open. You try.'

We both tried, and the umbrella suddenly bellied out, the spokes tore through the soaking cover; the wind danced its tatters; it wrangled above us in the wind like a ruined, mathematical bird. We tried to tug it down: an unseen, new spoke sprang through its ragged ribs. Leslie dragged it behind him, along the pavement, as though he had shot it.

A girl called Dulcie, scurrying to the Itch-pit, sniggered 'Hallo', and we stopped her.

'A rather terrible thing has happened,' I said to her. She was so silly that, even when she was fifteen, we had told her to eat soap to make her straw hair crinkle, and Les took a piece from the bathroom, and she did.

'I know,' she said, 'you broke your gamp.'

'No, you're wrong there,'
Leslie said. 'It isn't *our*
umbrella at all. It fell off the
roof. *You* feel,' he said. 'You
can feel it fell off the roof.'
She took the umbrella gingerly
by its handle.

'There's someone up there
throwing umbrellas down,'
I said. 'It may be serious.'

She began to titter, and then grew silent and anxious as Leslie said: 'You never know. It might be walking-sticks next.'

'Or sewing-machines,' I said.

'You wait here, Dulce, and we'll investigate,' Leslie said.

We hurried on down the street, turned a blowing corner and then ran.

Outside Rabiotti's cafe, Leslie said: 'It isn't fair on Dulcie.' We never mentioned it again.

A wet girl brushed by. Without a word, we followed her. She cantered, long-legged, down Inkerman Street and through Paradise Passage, and we were at her heels.

'I wonder what's the point in following people,' Leslie said, 'it's kind of daft. It never gets you anywhere. All you do is follow them home and then try to look through the window and see what they're doing and mostly there's curtains anyway. I bet nobody else does things like that.'

'You never know,' I said. The girl turned into St Augustus Crescent, which was a wide lamplit mist. 'People are always following people. What shall we call her?'

'Hermione Weatherby,' Leslie said. He was never wrong about

names. Hermione was fey and stringy, and walked like a long gym-mistress, full of love, through the stinging rain.

'You never know. You never know what you'll find out. Perhaps she lives in a huge house with all her sisters——'

'How many?'

'Seven. All full of love. And when she gets home they all change into kimonos and lie on divans with music and whisper to each other and all they're doing is waiting for somebody like us to walk in, lost, and then they'll all chatter round us like starlings and put us in kimonos too, and we'll never leave the house until we die. Perhaps it's so beautiful and soft and noisy—like a warm bath full of birds . . .'

'I don't want birds in my bath,' said Leslie. 'Perhaps she'll slit her throat if they don't draw the blinds. I don't care what happens so long as it's interesting.'

She slip-slopped round a corner into an avenue where the neat trees were sighing and the cosy windows shone.

'I don't want old feathers in the tub,' Leslie said. Hermione turned in at number thirteen, Beach-view.

'You can see the beach all right,' Leslie said, 'if you got a periscope.'

We waited on the pavement opposite, under a bubbling lamp, as Hermione opened her door, and then we tip-toed across and down the gravel path and were at the back of the house, outside an uncurtained window.

Hermione's mother, a round, friendly, owlish woman in a pinafore, was shaking a chip-pan on the kitchen stove.

'I'm hungry,' I said.

'Ssh!'

We edged to the side of the window as Hermione came into the kitchen. She was old, nearly thirty, with a mouse-brown shingle and big earnest eyes. She wore horn-rimmed spectacles and a sensible, tweed costume, and a white shirt with a trim bow-tie. She looked as though she tried to look like a secretary in domestic films, who had only to remove her spectacles and have her hair cherished, and be dressed like a silk dog's dinner, to turn into a dazzler and make her employer Warner Baxter, gasp, woo, and marry her; but if Hermione took off her glasses, she wouldn't be able to tell if he was Warner Baxter or the man who read the meters.

We stood so near the window, we could hear the chips spitting.

'Have a nice day in the office, dear? There's weather,' Hermione's mother said, worrying the chip-pan.

'What's *her* name, Les?'

'Hetty.'

Everything there in the warm kitchen, from the tea-caddy and the grandmother clock, to the tabby that purred like a kettle, was good, dull, and sufficient.

'Mr Truscott was something awful,' Hermione said as she put on her slippers.

'Where's her kimono?' Leslie said.

'Here's a nice cup of tea,' said Hetty.

'Everything's nice in that old hole,' said Leslie, grumbling. 'Where's the seven sisters like starlings?'

It began to rain much more heavily. It bucketed down on the black back yard, and the little comfy kennel of a house, and us, and the hidden, hushed town, where, even now, in the haven of the Marlborough, the submarine piano would be tinning 'Daisy', and the happy henna'd women squealing into their port.

Hetty and Hermione had their supper. Two drowned boys watched them enviously.

'Put a drop of Worcester on the chips,' Leslie whispered; and by God she did.

'Doesn't anything happen anywhere?' I said, 'in the whole wide world? I think the *News of the World* is all made up. Nobody murders no one. There isn't any sin any more, or love, or death, or pearls and divorces and mink‑coats or anything, or putting arsenic in the cocoa . . .'

'Why don't they put on some music for us,' Leslie said, 'and do a dance? It isn't every night they got two fellows watching them in the rain. Not *every* night, anyway!'

All over the dripping town, small lost people with nowhere to go and nothing to spend were gooseberrying in the rain outside wet windows, but nothing happened.

'I'm getting pneumonia,' Leslie said.

The cat and the fire were purring, grandmother time tick-tocked our lives away. The supper was cleared, and Hetty and Hermione, who had not spoken for many minutes, they were so confident and close in their little lighted box, looked at one another and slowly smiled.

They stood still in the decent, purring kitchen, facing one another.

'There's something funny going to happen,' I whispered very softly.

'It's going to begin,' Leslie said.

We did not notice the sour, racing rain any more.

The smiles stayed on the faces of the two still, silent women.

'It's going to begin.'

And we heard Hetty say in a small secret voice: 'Bring out the album, dear.'

Hermione opened a cupboard and brought out a big, stiff, coloured photograph album, and put it in the middle of the table. Then she and Hetty sat down at the table, side by side, and Hermione opened the album.

'That's Uncle Eliot who died in Porthcawl, the one who had the cramp,' said Hetty.

They looked with affection at Uncle Eliot, but we could not see him.

'That's Martha-the-woolshop, you wouldn't remember her, dear, it was wool, wool, wool, with her all the time; she wanted to be buried in her jumper, the mauve one, but her husband put his foot down. He'd been in India. That's your Uncle Morgan,' Hetty said, 'one of the Kidwelly Morgans, remember him in the snow?'

Hermione turned a page. 'And that's Myfanwy, she got queer all of a sudden, remember. It was when she was milking. That's your cousin Jim, the Minister, until they found out. And that's our Beryl,' Hetty said.

But she spoke all the time like somebody repeating a lesson: a well-loved lesson she knew by heart.

We knew that she and Hermione were only waiting.
Then Hermione turned another page. And we knew, by their secret smiles, that this was what they had been waiting for.

'My sister Katinka,' Hetty said.

'Auntie Katinka,' Hermione said. They bent over the photograph.

'Remember that day in Aberystwyth, Katinka?' Hetty said softly. 'The day we went on the choir outing.'

'I wore my new white dress,' a new voice said.

Leslie clutched at my hand.

'And a straw hat with birds,' said the clear, new voice.

Hermione and Hetty were not moving their lips.

'I was always a one for birds on my hat. Just the plumes of course. It was August the third, and I was twenty-three.'

'Twenty-three come October, Katinka,' Hetty said.

'That's right, love,' the voice said. 'Scorpio I was. And we met Douglas Pugh on the Prom and he said: "You look like a queen to-day, Katinka," he said. "You look like a queen, Katinka," he said. Why are those two boys looking in at the window?'

We ran up the gravel drive, and around the corner of the house, and into the avenue and out on to St Augustus Crescent. The rain roared down to drown the town. There we stopped for breath. We did not speak or look at each other. Then we walked on through the rain. At Victoria corner, we stopped again.

'Good night, old man,' Leslie said.

'Good night,' I said.

And we went our different ways.